The Tao of Po

with additional text by
Barbara Layman

studio **fun**

A **READER'S DIGEST** COMPANY

White Plains, New York • Montréal, Québec • Bath, United Kingdom

In a land of legends and a time of great awakening, an unassuming panda named Po skyrockets—literally—onto the kung fu scene. What he lacks in actual skill, discipline, and promise he more than makes up for in embracing the essence of the *Tao Te Ching*, the art of living and uncomplicated flow of the universe. Many kung fu masters train rigorously for decades in order to experience serenity, peacefulness, perspective, and generous spirit—the ultimate rewards of the *Tao*. But Po experiences awesomeness in everything naturally.

Po puts *excel* in excellent, *pro* in progress, and *light* in enlightenment. Big but balanced, the easy-going panda exhibits his elusive wisdom in every action because he is in true harmony with the *Tao*.

Master Shifu is bound by tradition. The Furious Five seek perfection. Mr. Ping desires remuneration. Tai Lung spawns destruction. Lord Shen covets domination. Kai hungers for ascension.

Meanwhile, Po simply is.

Before he becomes a master, Po visualizes himself among his kung fu heroes. He even trains with the Furious Five—in the form of wooden action figures—until his dream becomes reality. When uncompromising training leaves him beaten up, bruised, and mocked, Po revels in it all, concentrating on the singular truth that he's actually living his dream. As Oogway once taught, a thing is neither good nor bad. What matters is the attention we give it.

"And that's the not-so-secret secret behind the Tao of Po," Soothsayer explains as she and Po sit beneath Oogway's blossoming peach tree.

"Excuse me, the what-now of who-that?" asks Po who is just resting his eyes.

"*The Tao of Po.*"

"You mean me, the Dragon Warrior?"

"Yes, Po."

"*Cooool*! But, um, I know you're trying to be all mystical and kung fu–ey and stuff, but what exactly is *Tao* and why am I…of it?"

"Again…" Soothsayer sighs, "Tao is the art of living, the basic principle of the universe, and you do that so beautifully. In fact, better than most I'd say."

"Well, I do like living. Kind of a no-brainer, really. I mean, doesn't everybody?"

"Certainly, but not everyone knows *how* to live so fully and easily as you, Po. Struggle and frustration plague others' hearts. Whereas obstacles roll off your back as if you were a duck."

"Ooh! Master Duck is *awwwesooooome!*"

"As are you, Dragon Warrior. You desired to be a kung fu master and here you are. You yearned to train with the Furious Five. Done! You—what are you doing?"

"Uhh, eatnn dumplnns."

"Oh, wonderful example, Po! The *Tao Te Ching* imparts that there is no moment like the present, and you seized it beautifully!"

GULP!

"It just felt right…in my gut."

"Precisely!"

"Oh, I get it! My belly *presently* desired a dumpling so I *seized* it with my mouth!" Po thinks a moment. "Wait, *that's* how I became the Dragon Warrior?"

"More or less."

"That's what I thought…in my *mind*."

"Very good. And now others will learn from you so they may discover how to tap into their own Dragon Warrior."

"You mean their own inner awesomeness!"

"Yes, Po."

Po pauses momentarily, closing his eyes. "It is so," he says.

And so it is.

Like Po, we each have opportunities to draw from the awesomeness within and seize the grand moments that shape our destiny. So if you seek to discover who you are, take a lesson from Po: Be yourself. Follow your dreams. And live your truth.

The wisdom collected in this book will guide you along the path to your own inner awesomeness. Then, one day not far from now, you will feel so awesome you can't help but exclaim—in the manner of one famous kung fu master—"Skadoosh!"

Po, the fun-loving panda, dreams of performing kung fu with the Furious Five, China's most revered masters. But Po's adoptive father, Mr. Ping, expects his loving son to take over the family noodle shop.

Effortlessly in harmony with the *Tao Te Ching*—or, going with the flow of the universe—Po dutifully serves the noodles yet never stops dreaming. Po's destiny begins to take shape when Master Oogway predicts an old enemy, Tai Lung, will return. The sage tortoise then proclaims it is time to choose the Dragon Warrior, a master of great skill who will be granted the secrets of the universe contained in the sacred Dragon Scroll. For only the Dragon Warrior will be able to defeat Tai Lung.

The Furious Five's teacher, Master Shifu, holds a competition for his students to prove who is truly worthy. Super-psyched to see his idols perform in person and also help his dad's business, Po takes his noodle cart to the event. The exhausted panda arrives just as the gates close, but quick-thinking Po trades his cart for a chair and exploding fireworks—and soars into the stadium. He lands before Oogway, who mysteriously appoints Po as the Dragon Warrior!

The universe has spoken. Stunned at Oogway's decision, the Five and Shifu initially shun the awkward panda during training. But Po is ecstatic—his dream is coming true! Enthusiasm (and plentiful dumplings) carry Po through rigorous training.

When Tai Lung defeats the Furious Five, Shifu tells an anxious Po that he can be victorious with the power of the Dragon Scroll. But when Po unfurls it, only blank parchment is revealed. Dispirited, Po stares at his reflection in the empty scroll until he finally understands—the secrets of the universe and the power to defeat Tai Lung are *within him.*

Finally believing in himself, Po suddenly feels powerful…unstoppable…*awesome*. Mixing ingenuity, girth, and his favorite kung fu move, Po becomes the Dragon Warrior and single-paw-edly restores peace to the valley.

Of course, new challenges loom on the horizon….

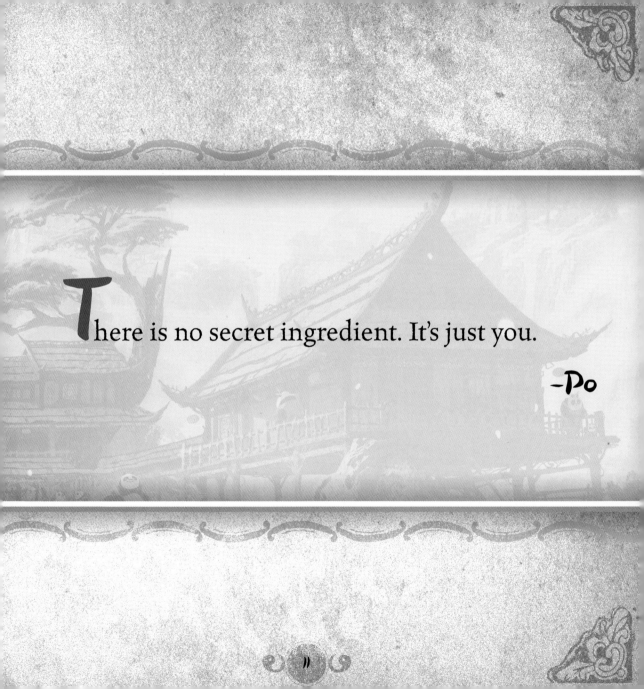

There is no secret ingredient. It's just you.

—Po

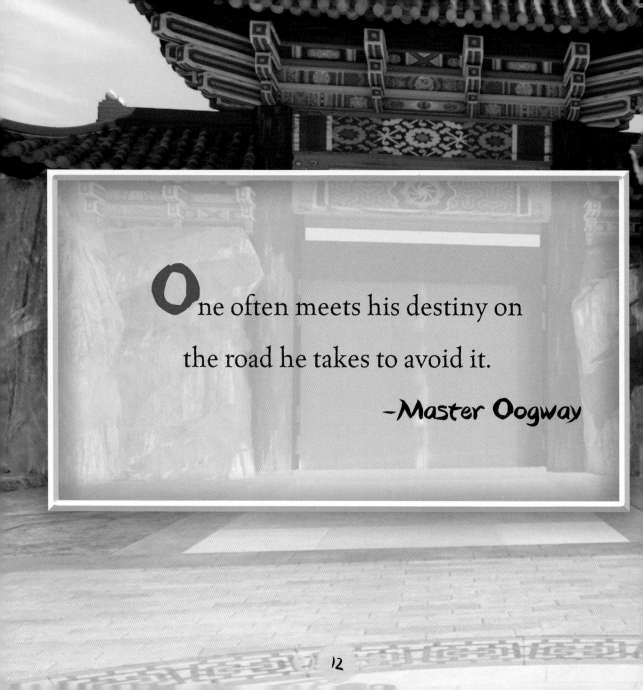

One often meets his destiny on the road he takes to avoid it.

—Master Oogway

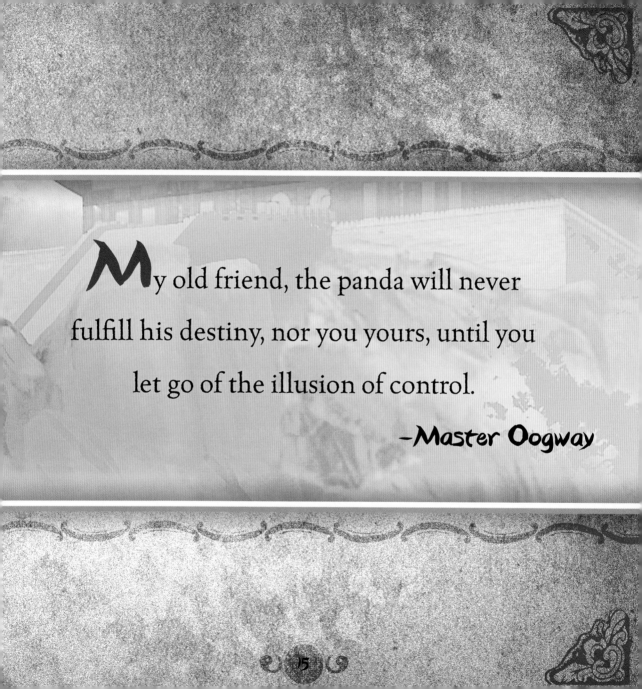

My old friend, the panda will never fulfill his destiny, nor you yours, until you let go of the illusion of control.

—Master Oogway

You just need to believe. Promise me, Shifu. Promise me you will believe.

-Master Oogway

To make something special, you just

have to believe it's special.

-Mr. Ping

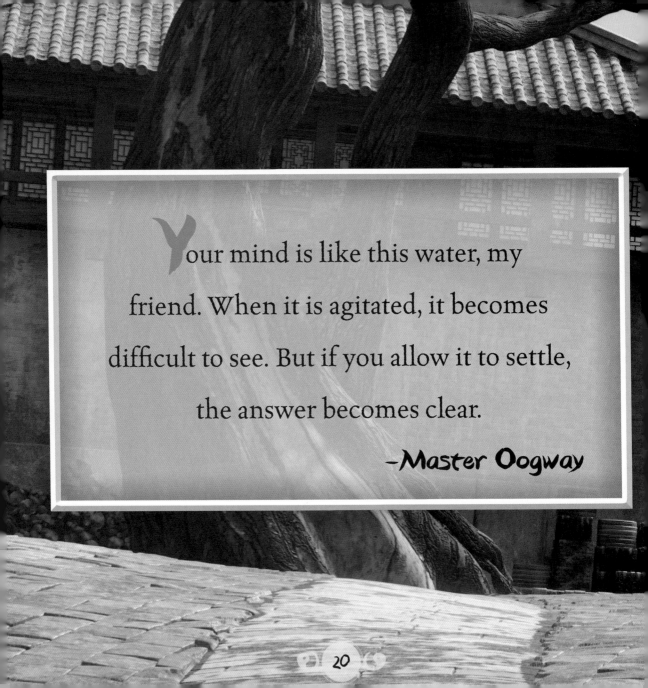

Your mind is like this water, my friend. When it is agitated, it becomes difficult to see. But if you allow it to settle, the answer becomes clear.

—Master Oogway

Quit, don't quit. Noodles, don't noodles. You are too concerned with what was and what will be. There is a saying: Yesterday is history, tomorrow is a mystery, but today is a gift. That is why it is called the present.

-Master Oogway

A real warrior never quits. Don't worry, Master, I will never quit!

-Po

KUNG FU PANDA 2

Po is living his dream as Dragon Warrior, protecting the Valley of Peace by battling bandits alongside his friends and fellow kung fu masters, the Furious Five. But the over-excited panda soon learns that kung fu fighting is only half the battle in becoming a true master.

Shifu explains that Po must achieve inner peace to now *harness* the flow of the universe. And Po will need it—for a new evil threatens the peace of all of China. Lord Shen, heir of the peacock clan, seeks to destroy kung fu tradition with a catastrophic cannon and rule supreme.

Long ago, when Shen's Soothsayer foretold that "a warrior of black and white" would defeat him, the foul fowl ordered the extermination of all pandas.

Years later, upon Po's first encounter with Shen's wolf henchmen, a symbol on the wolves' armor triggers a flashback of Po's mother. When Po asks where he came from, Mr. Ping lovingly explains that he adopted him after he found baby Po in a radish crate. There's little time for reflection, for Po and the Five must destroy the crackpot peacock's cannon before it's too late.

Confronting Shen, Po spies the same symbol on his plumage, recalling Shen's presence on the night he was separated from his parents. Po is shaken and captured but is rescued by Soothsayer who guides the uneasy panda to embrace his past.

Po's memory further reveals his mother hiding him in the crate, sheltering him from Shen's forces. Soothsayer also reminds Po that, despite the tragic past, he has lived a happy, fulfilling life—an awareness that helps Po finally achieve inner peace.

During the final battle with Shen, a fully focused Po musters his newfound understanding of the *Tao Te Ching* to redirect the cannon's blast against Shen's armada. Victorious, Po reunites with Mr. Ping, embracing him as his dad.

Meanwhile, unbeknownst to Po, his biological father is alive in a hidden village of pandas, and senses that his only son is also alive….

Remember Dragon Warrior, anything is possible when you have inner peace.

-Master Shifu

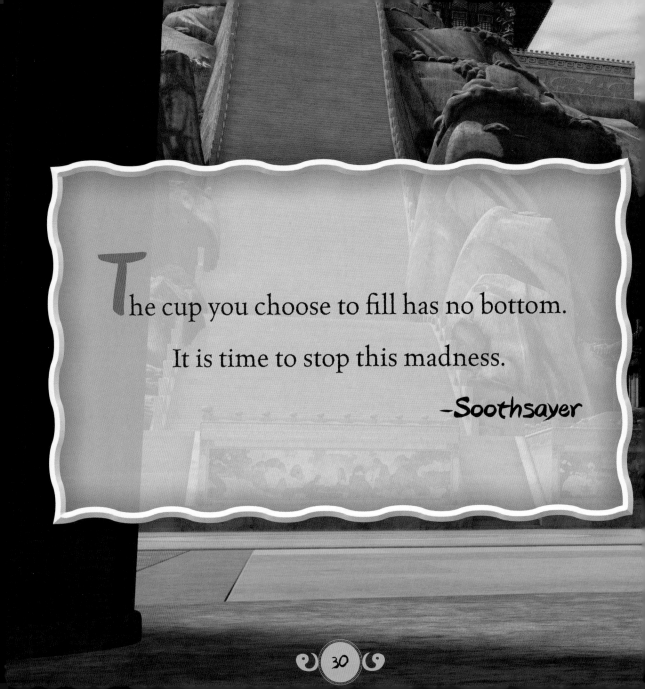

The cup you choose to fill has no bottom.

It is time to stop this madness.

—Soothsayer

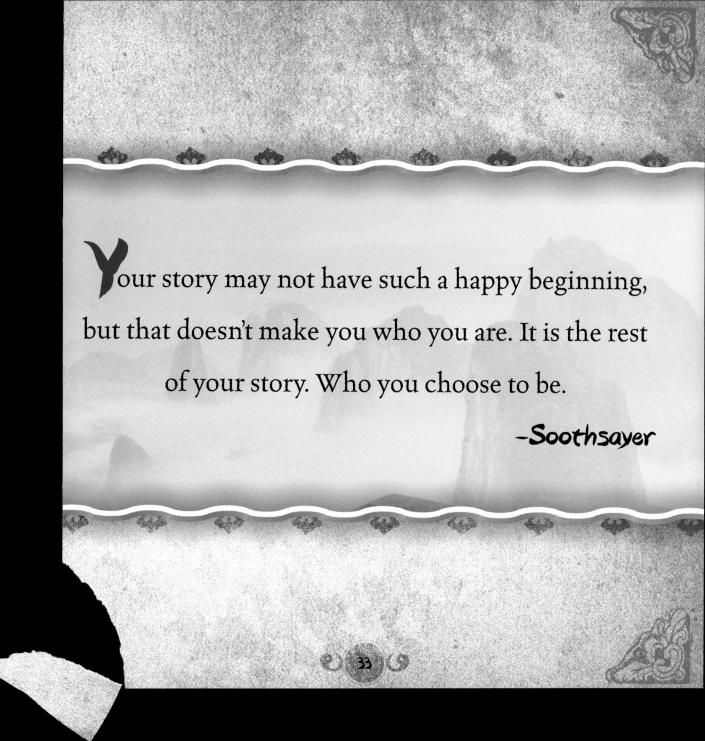

Your story may not have such a happy beginning, but that doesn't make you who you are. It is the rest of your story. Who you choose to be.

–Soothsayer

You gotta let go of that stuff from the past, 'cause it just doesn't matter. The only thing that matters...is what you choose to be now.

-Po

Nothing's unstoppable. Except for me, when I'm stopping you from telling me something's unstoppable!

—Po

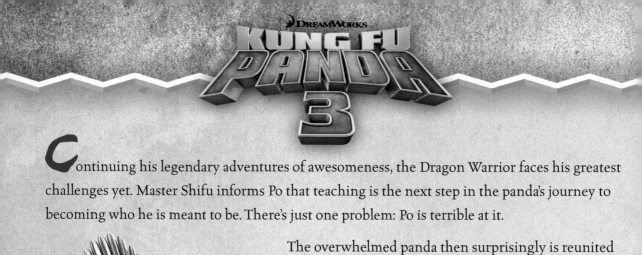

KUNG FU PANDA 3

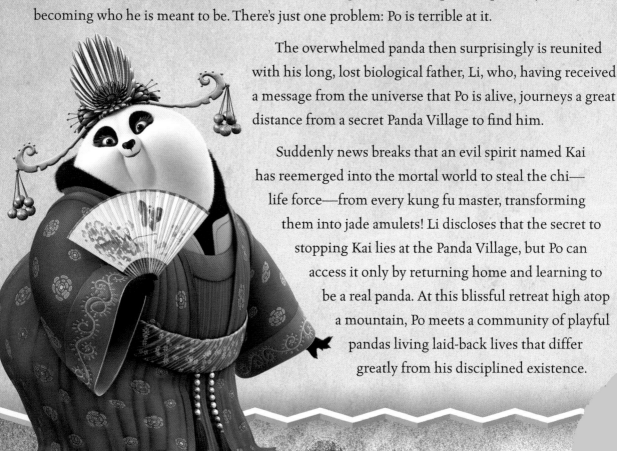

Continuing his legendary adventures of awesomeness, the Dragon Warrior faces his greatest challenges yet. Master Shifu informs Po that teaching is the next step in the panda's journey to becoming who he is meant to be. There's just one problem: Po is terrible at it.

The overwhelmed panda then surprisingly is reunited with his long, lost biological father, Li, who, having received a message from the universe that Po is alive, journeys a great distance from a secret Panda Village to find him.

Suddenly news breaks that an evil spirit named Kai has reemerged into the mortal world to steal the chi— life force—from every kung fu master, transforming them into jade amulets! Li discloses that the secret to stopping Kai lies at the Panda Village, but Po can access it only by returning home and learning to be a real panda. At this blissful retreat high atop a mountain, Po meets a community of playful pandas living laid-back lives that differ greatly from his disciplined existence.

Just as Po is finally feeling at one with his panda-ness, Tigress brings news that Kai has defeated Shifu and the rest of the Five—and is on his way to the Panda Village. Po refocuses on obtaining the means to defeat Kai, but Li is forced to admit he doesn't know the secret—he just wanted to keep his son safe at home. With Kai rapidly approaching, Po finally does the thing he thought he couldn't do—teach—as he trains the pandas how to fight alongside him.

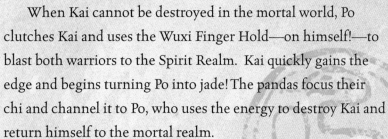

When Kai cannot be destroyed in the mortal world, Po clutches Kai and uses the Wuxi Finger Hold—on himself!—to blast both warriors to the Spirit Realm. Kai quickly gains the edge and begins turning Po into jade! The pandas focus their chi and channel it to Po, who uses the energy to destroy Kai and return himself to the mortal realm.

Now with *two* loving dads by his side, Po's journey comes full circle. By learning to embrace his innate wisdom, the embodiment of the *Tao Te Ching*, the Dragon Warrior finds his path, discovers who he truly is, and fulfills his destiny. Sweet!

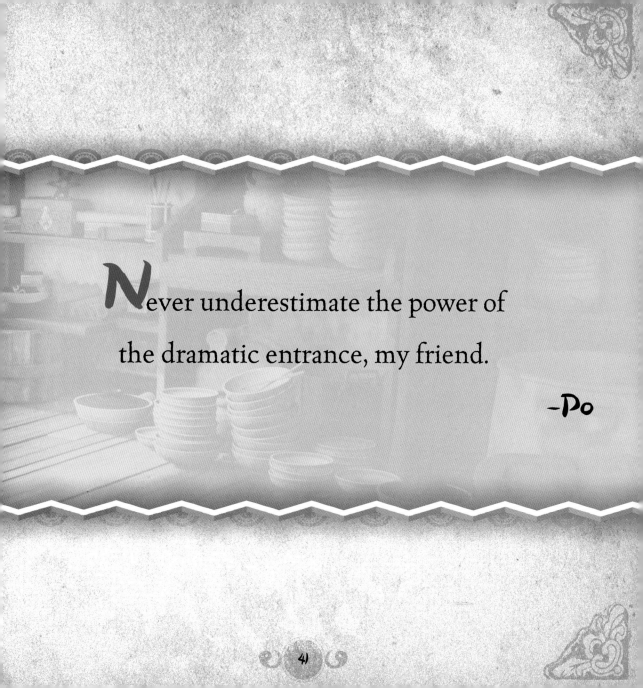

Never underestimate the power of the dramatic entrance, my friend.

—Po

Before the battle of the fist

comes the battle of the mind.

Hence…the dramatic entrance.

—Master Shifu

You're terrible at it today. But tomorrow… you'll still be terrible. The next day? Terrible. But someday, if you work hard, you might actually be not-so-terrible.

–Master Shifu

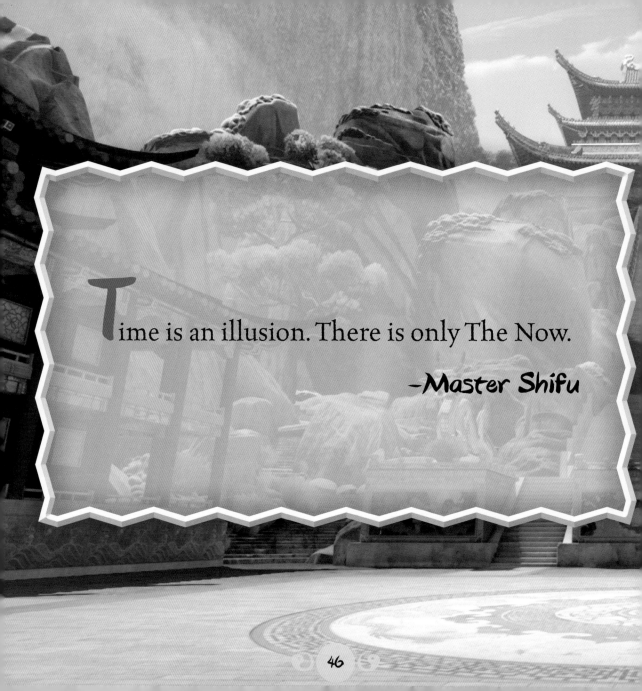

Time is an illusion. There is only The Now.

-Master Shifu

*E*verything changes. The only constant in life is change. For only by accepting change can you become who you are truly meant to be.

-Master Shifu

I don't have to become you! And you don't have to become me! We all just have to become the best us we can be!

–Po

There is always something more

to learn, even for a master.

-Master Shifu

Keep your center strong.

—Po